I Have An Angel of My Very Own

Written by: Patty F. Childs

Inspiring Voices books may be ordered through booksellers or by contacting:

Inspiring Voices
1663 Liberty Drive
Bloomington, IN 47403
www.inspiringvoices.com
1 (866) 697-5313

ISBN: 978-1-4624-1269-3 (sc)
ISBN: 978-1-4624-1270-9 (e)

Print information available on the last page.

Inspiring Voices rev. date: 5/6/2019

InspiringVoices

Who would have thought it,
Death would snatch you that day.
I wonder...
Did the Angels carry you away?

Did you hear the flutter
Of their majestic wings?
Or was it quiet, just silence,
You didn't hear anything.

Did you follow a light?
Did you feel afraid?
Or was it fun and exciting,
Like a big parade?

Were there loved ones waiting
Who'd gone on before?
Your Mom or your Dad,
And so many more.

Were there pets there in Heaven,
Like your dog, Old Blue?
I bet he came running
Cause he knew it was you!

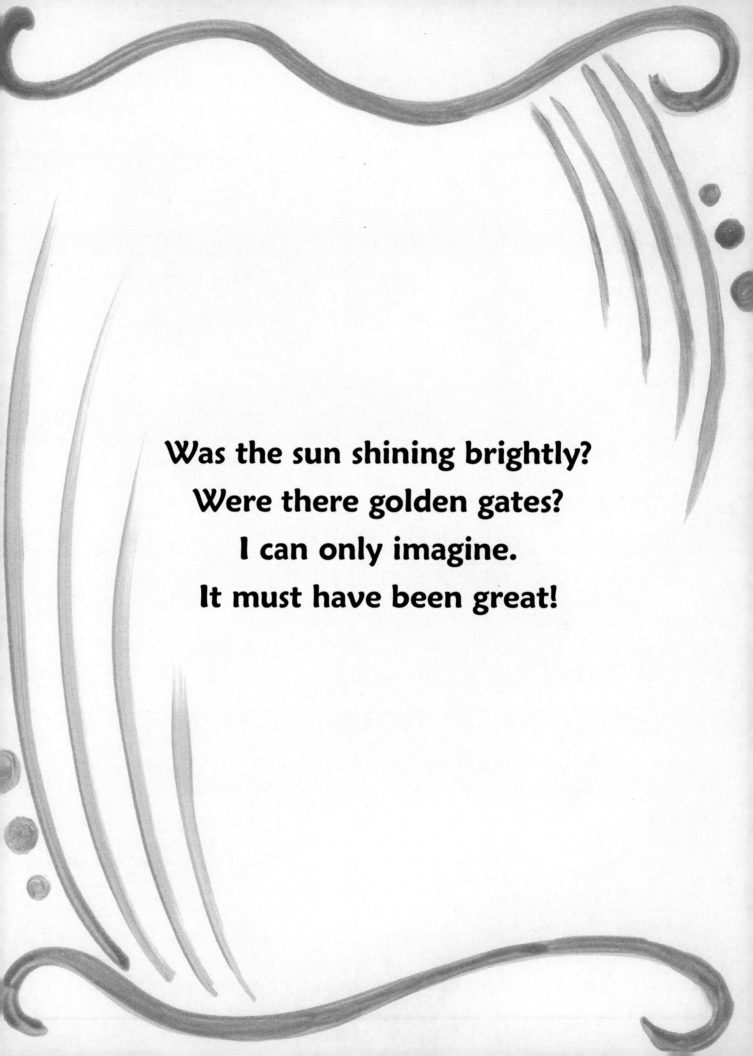

Was the sun shining brightly?
Were there golden gates?
I can only imagine.
It must have been great!

Do you wear a white robe?
Did they give you some wings?
Did you get a halo?
What an awesome thing!

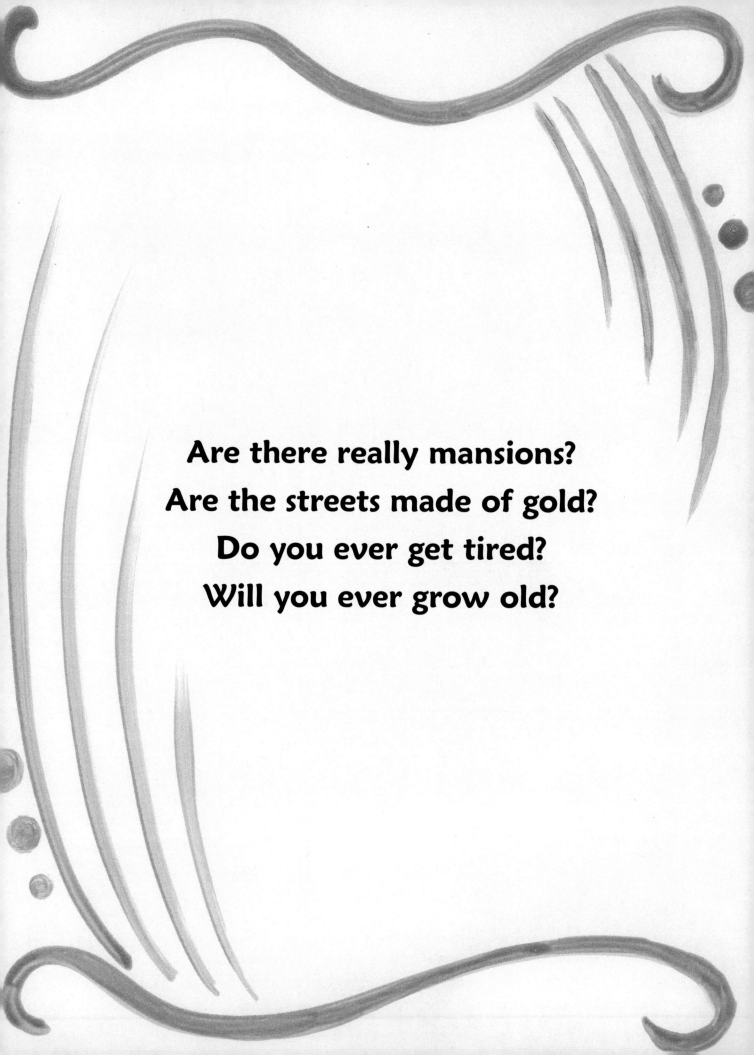

Are there really mansions?
Are the streets made of gold?
Do you ever get tired?
Will you ever grow old?

Do you blow a trumpet
In the Angel Band?
Did you talk with Jesus,
Or get to shake his hand?

Is there night time in Heaven?
Do you go to bed?

Do you get up early,
Or sleep in instead?

Please tell me the truth...
Is there any school?
Do you have to live
By the Golden Rule?

Are there really rewards
For our life here on earth?
Did you get a crown,
And what is it worth?

Is it like what we read
In the Bible's story?
Did you get to see God
And stand in His glory?

I miss you so much.
Will you still calm my fears?
I know you are happy,
Cause in Heaven there's no tears.

Don't worry about me,
I won't feel alone.
For I have an angel
Of my very own!

Printed in the United States
By Bookmasters